DEADLY TRAP

BY JOHN SAZAKLIS

ORCHARD

MEET THE TEAM:

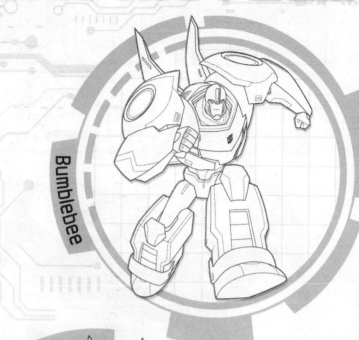

Bumblebee

Sideswipe

700042353479

ORCHARD BOOKS
Carmelite House
50 Victoria Embankment
London EC4Y 0DZ

First published as AUTOBOT WORLD TOUR in 2015 in the United States
by Little, Brown and Company

This edition published by Orchard Books in 2017

HASBRO and its logo, TRANSFORMERS, TRANSFORMERS ROBOTS IN
DISGUISE, THE LOGO and all related characters are
trademarks of Hasbro and are used with permission.

A CIP catalogue record for this book is available
from the British Library.

ISBN 978 1 40834 496 5

3 5 7 9 10 8 6 4 2

Printed in Great Britain

Orchard Books
An imprint of Hachette Children's Group
Part of The Watts Publishing Group Limited
An Hachette UK Company
www.hachette.co.uk

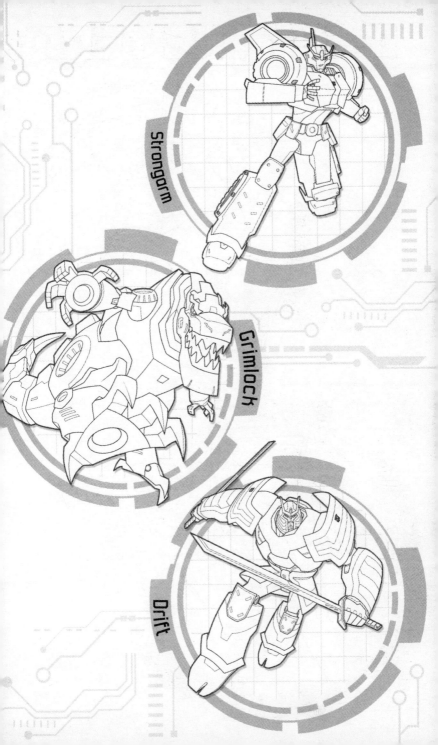

Strongarm

Grimlock

Drift

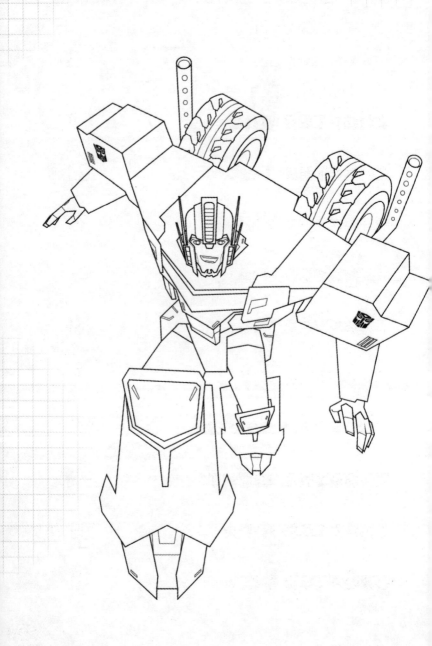

CONTENTS

FLICK TO SCROLL

STATUS REPORT: A prison ship from the planet Cybertron has crashed on Earth, and deadly robot criminals – the Decepticons – have escaped.

It's up to a team of Autobots to find them and get them back into stasis. Lieutenant Bumblebee, rebellious Sideswipe and police trainee Strongarm have taken the Groundbridge from Cybertron to Earth to track them down.

Along with bounty hunter, Drift, reformed Decepticon, Grimlock, and the malfunctioning pilot of the ship, Fixit, as well as the two humans who own the scrapyard where the ship crashed, Russell Clay and his dad, Denny, the robots in disguise must find the Decepticons, before they destroy the entire world ...

CHAPTER ONE

"YOU'RE GOING DOWN, YOU overgrown spark plug!" Sideswipe shouted, leaping from branch to branch. The headstrong young Autobot was in hot pursuit of a bug-like Decepticon who was crackling with electricity. "After I'm done with you," Sideswipe yelled, "you won't even be able to charge up a blinking tail-light!"

The two bots raced through the rainforest undergrowth, thousands of miles away from the scrapyard that served as the Autobots' base on Earth. Sideswipe's ninja-like acrobatics allowed him to keep pace easily with the swiftly flying Decepticon.

When Bumblebee and Optimus Prime had decided to assemble an away team to travel around Earth hunting down rogue Decepticons, Sideswipe had been the first to volunteer. Who wanted to sit around a scrapyard when there were rear axles to kick? As far as Sideswipe was concerned, he was more than a match for anybot – and eager to prove it.

The rest of his team trailed behind him: legendary Autobot leader Optimus Prime; stoic samurai Drift; Drift's Mini-Con students, Slipstream and Jetstorm; and the newest addition to the squad, Windblade.

"Hey, Slick, wait up!" Windblade shouted after Sideswipe. "We don't know what this Decepticon can do. The tree cover is so thick that we can't radio Fixit for any information." Windblade and Drift sliced through vines with their swords, clearing a path for Optimus and the Mini-Cons. "Let's hang back. No sense going into a fight blind."

"Are you kidding me?" Sideswipe yelled back, barely glancing over his shoulder at his team-mates. "Look at this puny bot. He can't be any more dangerous than a bug zapper!"

The electrified Decepticon let out a shrill buzzing noise in response to Sideswipe's insult. He stopped in his tracks and spread his shiny, metallic wings, revealing a vibrantly glowing green battery.

Sideswipe ground to a halt, narrowly avoiding a collision with the enemy bot.

"No one calls Shocksprocket 'puny' and gets away with it," the agitated Decepticon growled. "I'll show you what I can do, all right!"

Shocksprocket's battery pulsed with a radioactive green light. Sideswipe took a cautious step backwards. Windblade and the other bots kept their distance.

ZZZZZZaP!

The Decepticon let loose a massive arc of electricity, jolting Sideswipe and turning the damp soil under the Autobots' feet into a painful carpet of shocks! As the bots twisted in pain, Shocksprocket made a break for it.

"Into the trees!" Drift shouted, pulling himself off the ground and on to a sturdy branch. His two Mini-Cons scurried up nearby trees to join their master.

"Sideswipe's injured. We have to help him!" Windblade said. She leapt off the electrified ground and grabbed hold of the vines around her.

"I'll get him," Optimus said, grimacing through the discomfort of being shocked. "I'm too heavy to climb into the trees. You just – argh! – make sure that Decepticon doesn't – ouch! – escape!"

Steeling himself, Optimus stomped towards Sideswipe while Drift, Windblade and the Mini-Cons dashed through the trees in the direction of the rapidly fleeing Shocksprocket. Optimus hoisted the young bot into his arms as the final arcs of electricity died down around them.

"Sideswipe, are you all right?"

"Whoa," the young bot said, sparks dancing in front of his optics. "I need to throttle back on the Energon next time. I think I overcharged."

Optimus shook his head in disapproval. "Now we know what this Shocksprocket is capable of. Let's help the others take him down," Optimus said. "And this time, try not to provoke him." Sideswipe and Optimus shook off any remaining effects of their unexpected jolt and sprinted after their team-mates. The dense jungle foliage rendered their vehicle modes useless, giving Shocksprocket an advantage as he flitted between the tightly packed trees.

Before long, the Autobots were

reunited in a clearing bordered on three sides by trees and on one side by a jagged wall of rock.

"Nowhere to run, Decepticon!" Optimus roared. "Surrender!"

"I'm not the one who's trapped, Autobot bully!" Shocksprocket's battery started to hum, building up another massive charge.

"Quick, everyone, back into the trees!" Drift ordered.

"I'll grab Slipstream and Jetstorm," Windblade said, taking advantage of the open clearing to shift into her vehicle mode, a vertical takeoff and landing jet. Her turbines spun rapidly to life, lifting her above the treeline with the Mini-Cons clinging on below.

"Don't worry, getting bug-zapped gave me a plan!" Sideswipe said, yanking a thick branch off a giant tree. "These Earth plants don't seem to conduct electricity, which means they should be safe to use as ..."

Sideswipe leapt into the air towards Shocksprocket, bringing the heavy branch down onto the Decepticon's head.

THWACK!

"... a flyswatter!"

The hum of Shocksprocket's battery died down, and with it the radioactive green glow. Sideswipe dropped the branch next to the defeated Decepticon.

Drift and Optimus climbed out of the trees. Windblade and the Mini-Cons touched back down on solid ground.

"Letting you get attacked is a good
way to figure out a plan!" Windblade
said, changing back into her bot mode.

She cuffed Sideswipe on the shoulder affectionately. If bots could blush, Sideswipe would have been bright red.

"It looks like we have signal in this clearing," Optimus said, tapping at his communicator. "I'll tell Fixit to cross another Decepticon off the wanted list while you bots get Shocksprocket into stasis."

Fixit's eager face fizzed into view on Optimus's screen.

"Hello, friend-bots! Bumblebee, Strongarm and Grimlock are off chasing down another Decepticon signal. My, you all stay busy!" Fixit said. "I hope you are enjoying the jumble … rumble … jungle!"

Ever since Fixit had crashed to Earth in
the Alchemor prison ship, his speech
module had been broken, but his friends
wouldn't have him any other way.

Sideswipe pushed his way into the
frame, crowding Optimus's space.
"Actually, the heat and humidity are real
pains for my paint job. I'm worried my
good looks are going to rust!"

"Well, I've got good news for you,
then!" Fixit said with a smile. "Your next
destination won't be humid or hot – it'll
be freezing! It's approximately twenty-
nine thousand and twenty-nine feet above
sea level. Set your Groundbridge, you're
going to Mount Everest!"

CHAPTER TWO

"MOUNT EVEREST?" WINDBLADE said. "Fixit, you little bundle of loose screws, you better be kidding."

"What's so bad about some mountain?" Sideswipe asked. Windblade looked at the other bots for support, then slowly realised that they were just as unfamiliar with the famous mountain as Sideswipe was.

"I sometimes forget that not every bot has been on this planet as long as I have," she told them. "Mount Everest is one of the most extreme locations anywhere on Earth. Humans often try to climb it to prove their bravery. Some fail – permanently."

"Sounds dangerous," Sideswipe said, slinking closer to Windblade. "And I like danger."

"Cool your wheels, Slick," Windblade said, glaring at the young bot.

The typically silent Drift stepped forward. "As much as I regret agreeing with Sideswipe, he is correct in principle. We are much more durable than the inhabitants of this planet. I am confident that I can rise to the task." The dutiful Mini-Cons behind him nodded in agreement.

"I think you mean *we* can rise to the task, buddy," Sideswipe said.

Drift did not respond.

"Enough debate, Autobots," Optimus said, putting an end to the discussion.

"It is our sworn duty to protect this planet and the humans who call it home. That means going anywhere that we're needed." Optimus punched at the keys on his communicator, pulling up a larger hologram of Fixit for all the bots to see. "Fixit, what kind of threat have you identified?"

"Actually, sir, I can explain that!" A human boy pushed his way in front of Fixit. Russell Clay was the son of scrapyard owner Denny Clay. They were keeping the Autobots' presence a secret from the world, helping them to stay robots in disguise.

"I was watching my favourite show, *Beyond the Mysterious Unknown with Loren Fortean*, when I noticed—"

"Wait a minute," Sideswipe interrupted. "I thought your favourite show was *My Miniature Mustang*?"

"Jeez, Sideswipe, that was last week," Rusty replied. "Try to keep up. Anyway, as I was saying, I was watching the best show on television, *Beyond the Mysterious Unknown with Loren Fortean*, where this super-cool explorer, Loren Fortean, takes viewers 'beyond the veil of the known world-world-world!'"

"Optimus, your communicator is malfunctioning," Sideswipe said.

"Sideswipe! Stop interrupting me!" Rusty responded crossly. "Optimus's speaker isn't broken. That's just how the opening credits go: 'world-world-world', like an echo! Loren Fortean investigates all sorts of strange and mysterious occurrences, like crop circles, the Loch Ness monster, and why some junk food never goes bad.

And on his latest episode, he filmed a Decepticon!"

Optimus and the other bots exchanged concerned glances. "This is very serious, Rusty. If this Fortean human exposes our battle with the Decepticons, it could put humanity in grave danger."

"That's the best part, though," Rusty said. "Loren Fortean has no idea that it's a bot! Grimlock and I can recognise a Cybertronian a mile away – or on a TV screen, anyway – but the show's producers think they've found something else – a yeti!"

Rusty's enthusiasm was met with more blank stares from the bots.

"I'm not familiar with that Earth animal species," Optimus told him.

"That's because it doesn't exist," Rusty replied. "Or maybe it does, but we don't have proof yet. It's like a big white ape that lives in the Himalayan mountains. Only this one isn't an ape at all; it was definitely a Decepticon."

Windblade frowned as she considered what Rusty had said. "I know you trust the humans, Optimus," she said, "and I respect their contributions to our mission, but you're asking us to risk our sparks based on a human child thinking he saw something in a split-nanocycle frame of a remote audio/video signal. For all we know, this Fortean human has doctored the footage for attention."

"No!" Rusty said, getting defensive.

"Loren Fortean live-streams all his episodes, so viewers know we're getting a real look at the world beyond-beyond-beyond ..."

Sideswipe chuckled. "Hey, Fixit, Rusty's starting to sound like you!"

Fixit frowned.

"Actually, sir, I was able to verify Russell Clay's suspicions," the Mini-Con added. "To an extent, anyway. Our systems can't scan for accurate signals from this distance, but based on Russell's description and a scan of the footage, it looks like it may be a Decepticon called Abominus."

Windblade slapped her palm to her forehead. "Scrap!"

"You know him, Windy?" Sideswipe

asked, pointing at the hologram Fixit had provided. Abominus was a bulky, long-limbed, ape-like Decepticon, with a blindingly white paint job. His face was framed with armour plating that gave him more than a passing resemblance to an albino orangutan.

"First, don't call me 'Windy'," Windblade replied. "Second, yes, unfortunately I do. Eons ago, before I came to Earth, I helped to arrest him. Abominus is a hermit and a technical genius. He's obsessed with living off the grid and is willing to build any weapons he needs to defend his stronghold. He'll blast anyone who even looks at his bunker the wrong way, and he has a real problem with authority."

Sideswipe sidled up next to Drift and whispered into his audio receptor. "Good thing we're not bringing Strongarm with us then, right?" Once again, Drift ignored the young Autobot's comments.

Rusty's face reappeared on the hologram. "You have to protect Loren Fortean and his crew before this bad bot blows them all up!"

Optimus and the other bots exchanged solemn nods, with the exception of Sideswipe, who was unable to hide his excitement at the prospect of another daring adventure.

The Autobot leader reassured Rusty that everything was going to be OK. "Do not worry, Rusty. We'll apprehend

Abominus before he can harm Fortean
and his crew – or expose our existence to
the world!"

CHAPTER THREE

WHILE OPTIMUS AND THE AWAY team locked the rainforest rabble-rouser Shocksprocket in stasis and prepared to travel across the world, Bumblebee, Strongarm and Grimlock pursued a threat much closer to home. Just a few short miles away from their scrapyard headquarters, the bots were closing in on a Decepticon signal that was moving at a glacial pace.

"Sir, I have a bad feeling about this," Strongarm said to Bumblebee. A cadet from Cybertron, Strongarm loved rules and order. She took the cautious route every time – and always held it over Sideswipe's head when his riskier decisions came back to bite him in the tailpipe. "A signal this close to the command centre should have shown up weeks ago," she said, "unless the Decepticon has been perfectly still since the crash."

Grimlock stomped up next to Bumblebee and Strongarm. While Bumblebee and Strongarm had convenient Earth vehicle modes that allow them to get around inhabited areas without arousing suspicion, Grimlock's other mode was a fearsome Dinobot, meaning he had to stay out of human sight.

"Maybe a giant piece of the ship landed right on his stabilisers. *BOOM! CRASH!*" Grimlock said, exaggerating the sound effects. "And this bot's been surviving on scrap metal and Energon leaks, waiting for one of his evil buddies to come and rescue him!"

"Grimlock has a good point, Strongarm …" Bumblebee replied, zooming along in his yellow-and-black sports car mode. "If this signal does belong to an injured Decepticon, we have a responsibility to repair him before we lock him in stasis. These criminals deserve their sentences, but that doesn't mean we can neglect their diagnostics."

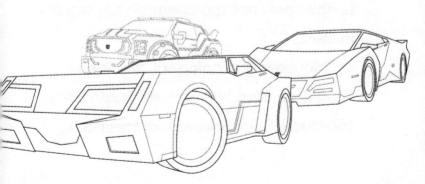

The Autobot trio rushed through the woods at a fast pace. Before long, they arrived at the source of the signal: a cracked stasis pod wedged between a tumble of fallen tree trunks and debris from the ship. Strongarm changed from her police cruiser form into bot mode, pulled out her blaster and ducked behind a tree to cover her team-mates.

"Sir," Strongarm whispered, "do you see anything?"

Bumblebee darted his optics around the crash site. The signal definitely led to this spot, but there was no Decepticon in sight.

"Negative. I'm going in," Bumblebee whispered back. "Watch my back!" The courageous Autobot leader sprinted

towards the pod, blaster in hand.
Bumblebee peeked over the rim and
through the shattered lid to find … a
Decepticon lying in wait!

"Freeze!" Bumblebee shouted, pointing
his blaster at the prone bot. The
Decepticon had a large, round face and
elongated arms, ending in a trio of
dangerously sharp claws. Even with the
commotion, his optics remained closed.
He'd been lying in place for so long that
moss had begun to grow on his exterior.

"Step out of the pod with your, uhh,
really pointy claws where I can see
them," Bumblebee shouted.

But the Decepticon gave no response.
Strongarm and Grimlock crept up to join
their leader. Grimlock lifted a massive

finger and poked the stasis chamber.

"Hello, anyone home in there?" he bellowed. "Wake up, you heap of junk!" The Dinobot pushed on the chamber with more force, rocking it back and forth. Still nothing from the Decepticon.

"Sir," Strongarm said in hushed tones, "maybe this prisoner was deactivated in the crash." The trio of Autobots leaned over the stasis pod, considering Strongarm's assessment. Before Bumblebee could agree, however, the Decepticon's optics slowly widened.

"Good morning, bro-bots," he said. He opened his mouth in a wide, yawn-like motion as he looked around. "That power-down was exactly what I needed. I feel so ... relaxed."

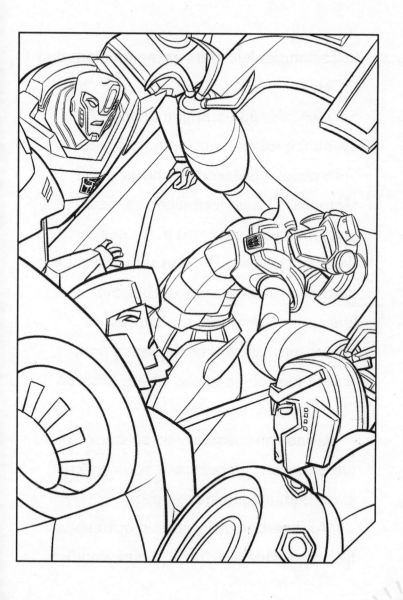

The three Autobots exchanged puzzled looks.

"Uhh, should I stomp him now?" Grimlock asked.

"Whoa, who needs to do any stomping?" the Decepticon replied. He stretched his long arms in a slow arc, flexing his claws. The Autobots all took a defensive step backwards, but the Decepticon only dug the impressive blades into the rim of the stasis pod, pulling himself up into a sitting position. "Let's all just, like, chill."

Strongarm steadied her blaster. "You're under arrest, Decepticon. You can 'chill' in an undamaged stasis pod."

"Yo, bro-bot, why do you have to harsh my vibe like that?" he responded.

This strange new Decepticon was really trying Grimlock's patience.

"C'mon, Bee, what are we waiting for?" he grumbled. "Let me stomp this guy already! Listening to him makes me feel like I've got brain rust!"

Before the Autobots could make a move – stomping or otherwise – the Decepticon's optics started to flash with a kaleidoscope of colours. Strongarm, Bumblebee and Grimlock were helpless to look away.

"I tried to do this the chill way, bro-bots, but you forced my hand," the Decepticon said, optics still flashing. "Now repeat after me: 'I don't wanna arrest my buddy Brakepad.'"

"I don't wanna arrest my buddy Brakepad," the bots chanted in unison.

"I'm feeling super lazy. Let's all just, like, hang out," Brakepad said.

The Autobots mimicked his words, drawling lazily. "Let's all just hang out."

Brakepad's optics stopped flashing, and the Autobots slumped to the ground as if their power had been drained. With the heroic bots temporarily incapacitated, Brakepad slowly crawled away from the crash site, heaving his body forward using his massive claws.

By the time the Autobots noticed, the Decepticon was long gone – and so was their energy!

CHAPTER FOUR

THOUSANDS OF MILES AWAY, A Groundbridge portal opened up on the side of a snowy mountain. Optimus, Windblade, Sideswipe, Drift and his Mini-Cons stepped through it, finding themselves at the base of a massive incline.

"Whoa, can you imagine surfing down that slope?" Sideswipe asked, miming a surfer's stance.

"I can imagine you ending up a pile of spare parts if you tried it, Slick," Windblade replied. "This is as far up the mountain as I can safely take us with the Groundbridge. The rest of the way we have to climb."

Optimus tapped at his communicator and pulled up a fuzzy image of Fixit.

"Hello again, friends!" the Mini-Con's voice came through the static. "You won't get much single ... shingle ... SIGNAL on the mountain, but I wanted to warn you about—" The feed disappeared. Optimus shook his communicator, bringing it back to life. "... could trigger ... valanches, so be caref ... when you ... or cause ... disaster! Good luck!"

"Yeesh, that wasn't ominous at all," Sideswipe said.

"Our vehicle forms won't be of much use here," Optimus explained, briefing the team. "The terrain is too steep and rocky for our wheeled modes, and the crosswinds are too furious for Windblade

to safely manoeuvre as a jet plane. We'll
need to use our winter camoflage to blend
in with the snow and prevent the human
television crew from filming us. Our job is
to get in, take down Abominus and make
sure the humans make it back down the
mountain safely."

The bots put on their winter camoflage,
instantly replacing their vibrantly coloured
paint jobs with white-and-grey mottling
that concealed them against the icy
landscape.

"Do you want to hold down the fort
here, sir?" Windblade asked Optimus.
"The climb is going to get more
treacherous as we go."

"I'll be fine, soldier," Optimus snapped
back. Optimus Prime had been weakened

in a recent battle, sacrificing part of his
power to save the planet. Although he
wouldn't admit it to the other bots, he
was feeling self-conscious about his
diminished strength. Windblade was
doing her best to keep an eye on her
respected commander while he returned
to full power.

With the plan clear, the bots began
their trek up the huge mountain.
Fixit's long-range signal might not
reach this remote location, but the bots'
close-range sensors – and Windblade's
impressive intuition – told them that a
Decepticon was nearby in one direction:
up. As for the humans, the bots just had
to keep their optics peeled.

What started as a hike soon turned

into a climb, with the bots digging their hands into the mountainside to pull themselves up and along. "You know, Windy really made this sound more extreme," Sideswipe said, pulling himself over a ledge. "It's actually kind of … boring?"

"We're still close to the base of the mountain, Slick," Windblade replied. "You'll be begging for these easy slopes once we reach the summit."

As the incline steepened, Drift and his Mini-Cons took the lead, using their weapons to carve easier handholds into the rock. The further up the mountain they climbed, the heavier it began to snow, blanketing the bots in a thick white haze and obscuring their vision. Drift pulled himself over another ledge – and came face-to-face with a laser turret!

ZAP!

Drift barely dodged the blast, slipping to the side behind a snow bank. The turret pivoted to Drift's hiding place. The Autobot shouted down at his team-mates to stay below the ledge.

"Drift, what's happening?" Optimus
yelled as another laser blast cut through
the heavy snow. "We're
coming up!"

"No!" Drift shouted
back, nimbly dodging yet
another blast. Drift leapt
through the snow and
sliced the turret in two
with his blade. Optimus,
Sideswipe, Windblade and
the Mini-Cons heard the crunch of the
metal being cleaved and climbed up to
make sure Drift was OK.

"Scrud, that looks like Abominus's
handiwork, all right," Windblade said,
inspecting the defensive weaponry.

She had to shout to be heard over the rush of snow and wind. "This must mean we're getting closer. He probably has this entire section of the mountain booby-trapped!"

Sideswipe looked back over the ledge they had just climbed. It would be a long way down if one of Abominus's traps sent the bots tumbling off the mountain. A very long way down.

"There's no way we can find all his traps in conditions like this," Optimus shouted. "We need to pick up the pace and disable them at the source, before that human Rusty watches on the television stumbles into one!"

Back on the outskirts of Crown City, Rusty flipped channels on the vintage television his dad had installed in the diner they called home. Denny Clay was fussing around with retro soundtracks on an antique record player in the other room, filling the scrapyard with a chase theme, romantic interludes and horror music.

"Can you turn it down, Dad?" Rusty shouted, not budging from his place on the sofa. "Or at least pick a record? It sounds like I'm about to be attacked by a masked murderer on a date to the racetrack."

Denny poked his head in. "That sounds like a bodacious movie. I wish it existed! But if the sound is bothering you, I just got a box of novelty oversized sunglasses that I can polish instead." Denny pulled a huge pair of glasses from behind his back and held them against his face. "How cool are these babies?"

"Real cool, Dad." Rusty kept flipping channels, unenthused by his dad's new find. He was surprised when he landed on a bonus episode of *Beyond the Mysterious Unknown with Loren Fortean*.

"Good afternoon, faithful viewers," Loren Fortean said, decked out in cold-weather gear and holding the mic close to his face to block the wind. "It's your host, Loren Fortean, live-streaming a very important moment from … beyond the mysterious unknown!"

Rusty leaned forward, eyes glued to the screen.

"Just moments ago, my crew and I got

a glimpse at something incredible ... we
have spotted a yeti! In fact it was what
we believe to be an entire family of yeti
scaling Mount Everest. Unfortunately, we
didn't catch them on film, but we do have
a strange phenomenon to share with

you, my most loyal followers."

Fortean's cameraman panned upward, zooming in on a cliff blurred by raging snow. As the camera focused, a massive blast of red laser light shot through the snow, followed by another one and then a small explosion. The heavy snow made it impossible to make out anything else.

"Are the yetis performing some sort of strange, electronic dance ceremony?" Fortean asked as the camera returned to his face. "Have they mastered the art of the laser light show? Don't fret over these questions, faithful audience. I, Loren Fortean, am dedicated to sharing the truth with you! My crew and I are diverting from our course to track down the source of these lights. Tune in soon

for more ... *Beyond the Mysterious
Unknown with Loren Fortean!*"

Rusty exhaled, realising he'd been
holding his breath throughout the entire
segment.

"Uh-oh. I've got a bad feeling about
this. Those aren't yetis ... it's the
Autobots!"

CHAPTER FIVE

"FIXIT, WE NEED TO RADIO THE bots!" Rusty shouted, running into the command centre.

"Which ones, Russell Clay?" Fixit asked. "How nice that our team has expanded enough that I can ask that! Like one big Autobot family!"

"The away team – Optimus and Windblade," Rusty clarified. "I was just watching *Beyond the Mysterious Unknown with Loren Fortean*, and his camera crew have picked up some sort of laser fire. Either the bots are in danger of being attacked or they're in danger of being spotted by Loren Fortean – or both!"

Fixit dutifully punched away at his command console. But the communicator logo just spun and spun, unable to find a signal.

"I am sorry. The atmospheric conditions surrounding the away team are too intense. Optimus's communicator isn't picking up my message."

Rusty scrunched up his face in thought. "Wait a minute, if Cybertronian technology can't get through the bad weather, how is Loren Fortean live-streaming from the same location as the bots?"

"Hmm, that is curious," the Mini-Con replied, returning to his screen. "Let me see if I can zero in on this human's signal instead ... Aha, got it! It appears that your television human has an extensive series of relays placed around the mountain, amplifying his transmission strength. He's leaving one every hundred feet or so." Rusty shot Fixit a hopeful look, but the Mini-Con shook his head sombrely. "I can hack into it, but not without alerting the humans. Our friends are on their own!"

"Tell me you got that, Ernie," Loren Fortean said, dropping the mic.

"Sure did, boss," Ernie, the cameraman, replied. "You can see those laser lights real well."

"Not the lights, you brute," Fortean snapped. "I just had my teeth whitened, and I was trying to show them off during that segment." Despite the brutal wind and punishing cold, Fortean still managed to flash a Hollywood-ready gigawatt smile. His pearly white teeth perfectly matched the swirling snow. "My agent said it'd look good to the producers, help show them I'm ready for a better time slot than these commercial-length fillers they have me doing now."

Fortean, Ernie and their mountaineering guide, Brigadier Wilson, packed up their hefty equipment.

"Humph, do you even care about these missing links you're chasing after?" Brigadier Wilson asked, slinging a pack over his burly shoulders. Wilson knew the mountain like the back of his well-worn hand and he wasn't impressed with Loren's Hollywood foolishness. "Seems to me you just like the attention. And I'm betting these lights you think you saw were just tricks of the sun flashing off the ice."

"Of course I care," Fortean replied. "But I've done twenty-six episodes without actually finding anything and the studio is getting restless. This expedition is my last shot. Hiring you and funding all of these live-streaming relays cost a small fortune. If I don't come back with proof of something, I'm washed up, finished, kaput!" Fortean traded his expensive new smile for an exaggerated frown. "That's why we have to find whatever's shooting off those lights – and make sure I look ready for prime-time when we do."

Brigadier Wilson shook his head disapprovingly, drove another signal relay into the frozen ground, and began the trek further up to the summit.

Higher up the mountain, Drift and his Mini-Cons, Sideswipe, Optimus and Windblade had resumed their climb. Since stumbling across the first ambush, the Autobots had sliced through two more laser turrets, blasted a hidden nest of armour-piercing nanodrones, and narrowly dodged a set of spinning saw blades equipped with nova-hot heated tips.

"So climbing this thing is a big deal to humans?" Sideswipe asked. "If you factor out Abominus's toys, it seems pretty easy to me."

Windblade scoffed. "Keep telling yourself that, Slick. Won't seem so easy if you slip and end up tumbling into a crevasse full of ice spikes where we couldn't reach you. Over time, the cold would slowly bring your gears to a halt. After a few substantial snowfalls, you'd be lost for ever, just another forgotten part of the mountain."

"Wow, dramatic much?" Sideswipe responded, wincing at Windblade's grim imagination. "I could do this blindfolded, with a bad case of carburettor congestion." To prove his skill, the headstrong young bot swung his lower half up and landed on a rocky outcropping ahead of the other bots. "Boom!" he shouted.

As Sideswipe struck a triumphant pose, the mountain around him started to rumble. His optics darted around, prepared for a fight with another one of Abominus's traps. Drift, Optimus, Windblade and the Mini-Cons joined the young bot on the rock shelf, their weapons drawn.

Optimus warned the other bots to prepare themselves, but there was no target in sight. Instead the rumbling noise increased, as if a speeding train was bearing down on their location.

"Wait a nanocycle," Windblade said, her audio receptors listening attentively to the growing vibration. "I don't think that's the sound of a trap – I think Sideswipe just triggered an avalanche!"

Windblade barely had time to warn the other bots before they were engulfed in a rushing torrent of heavy snow and falling rocks, knocking them all completely off the cliff!

"Scrud!" Sideswipe yelled, tumbling head over treads as he plummeted down the mountainside. The quick-acting bot jammed his blades into the rock to slow his descent. He blinked through the barrage to see Windblade flying past in her aeroplane mode.

Windblade was struggling against the heavy wind, but she was managing to fly. "Grab hold!" she shouted at Optimus's tumbling form. Before he had sacrificed a portion of his spark to protect Earth, Optimus would have been the one

heroically rescuing his team-mates. Now he was the one who needed saving! But he was far too heavy for Windblade, and they both began to fall. "You're too big! I'm sorry, Optimus!"

Windblade barely managed to steer them away from the crushing avalanche and the falling debris. Her quick thinking allowed them to crash into a bank of snow on the other side of the danger.

The disaster ended as quickly as it had begun. As the snow cleared, the Autobots looked around to take stock of their team-mates. Windblade and Optimus had landed on stable ground far below. Drift and Sideswipe were both clinging to the side of the mountain with their blades jammed firmly into the rocks.

Jetstorm was clinging on to his master's back – but the other Mini-Con, Slipstream, was nowhere to be found!

CHAPTER SIX

WHILE THE AWAY TEAM RISKED their sparks, the home team of Bumblebee, Strongarm and Grimlock could barely muster the energy to trudge back to the scrapyard. They'd faced Energon vampires before, but the strange Decepticon Brakepad had left the bots with an entirely new sensation: laziness.

"We're back, I guess," Bumblebee mumbled, walking through the main gate. Fixit and Rusty rushed over to greet the bots and update them on the laser light spotting and signal issues.

"Bee!" Rusty exclaimed. "There's so much to tell you. So I was watching the show *Beyond the—*"

"Whoa," Strongarm said, cutting him off. "You are talking *way* too fast, Rusty. You're really bumming me out. What's the rush?"

Rusty and Fixit looked at each other with concern. Strongarm normally stuck to the rules rigidly, following protocol to a fault. Since when did she say things like 'bummed out'?

"Bee, what's wrong with Strongarm?" Rusty asked. "Did she get possessed by a ghost-bot or something?"

Bumblebee waved off Rusty's questions. "You humans are *way* too tense. You need to learn how to relax."

"But, sir, the away team is currently in one of the most dangerous natural locations on this planet, hunting a known criminal without any way to contact us," Fixit reminded his leader. "All while attempting to avoid television crews and exposing our existence to the human popsicle ... pinnacle ... POPULACE!"

"Eh, sounds like a normal day around here," Grimlock chimed in, stomping his way past the gathering. "Boot me up if anything really interesting happens. I'm going to enjoy some rest mode until then."

"Wait, what happened to the Decepticon you were hunting down?" Rusty asked, puzzled by his friends' behaviour. "Did you catch him? Where is he?"

"What does it matter to you?" Strongarm responded.

"Yeah," Bumblebee added. "We catch them and they just escape again. Might as well make it easier on all of us and stop trying."

At this comment, Rusty was ready to tear out his hair. Something was clearly very wrong with his friends. "Can you at least tell us his name before you all power down?"

Bumblebee mumbled an answer before he and Strongarm wandered off to follow Grimlock. "Seemed like he'd be a chill bro-bot to kick it with some time. I think his name was Brakepad."

"Oh my," Fixit whispered to Rusty. "That explains everything."

As Strongarm, Bumblebee and Grimlock
got situated around the scrapyard,
settling in for the Autobot equivalent of a
lazy mid-afternoon nap, Rusty grabbed
his father and followed Fixit to the
command centre. The hardworking
Mini-Con typed away at the console and
pulled up the profile for Brakepad.

"So he's the reason the bots are acting
so funny?" Denny asked, getting up to
speed on what's going on. "He looks
dangerous with those giant claws of his."

"Oh, those claws are just for show,"
Fixit responded. "That's why they're so
shiny and sharp – he never uses them in
battle. Brakepad was a very successful
thief back on Cybertron. His optics emit
a powerful laser light that drains bots of

their Energon. He gives everyone a powerful feeling of laziness that takes several cycles to dissipate."

"That explains why Bee and the others don't seem to care about anything," Rusty said. "They must have found Brakepad and had their energy sapped!"

"So how do we snap the bots out of it and make sure this doesn't happen the next time they try to capture Brakepad?" Denny asked.

Fixit knitted his optics together in thought and resumed tapping away at his console. "Aha!" he exclaimed eventually.

"Did you find something?" Rusty asked excitedly.

"Yes!" Fixit responded. "The prisoner

manifest includes instructions on how to dampen Brakepad's powers. There's a simple machine that loops the signals he gives off and puts *him* into a deep sleep instead of affecting other bots."

"That's perfect!" Denny replied. "How do we get started?"

Fixit frowned. "We would need several component parts that aren't available in this solar system. Fortunately, it looks like Brakepad's signal hasn't moved far from his original pod. His laziness is legendary. It's unlikely he will become a threat to Crown City before Bumblebee, Strongarm and Grimlock shake off the effects of his powers. Although they won't be able to get close to him again without getting lazy all over again ..."

Rusty looked at his dad for a moment. "Fixit, did you say that Brakepad never uses his sharp claws and is famous for being slow?"

"I did, Russell Clay. He is only an effective thief because other bots can't resist his power-sapping vision."

"So a bot that couldn't see him would be immune, right?"

"That seems to make sense, yes," Fixit replied.

"Dad, you may not like this," Rusty said, "but I think I have a plan for how the two of us can capture this Decepticon. And we're going to need your new toys and a gallon of black paint to pull it off!"

CHAPTER SEVEN

BACK ON THE MOUNTAIN, DRIFT
and Sideswipe withdrew their swords from
the cliff wall and dropped down to reunite
with Windblade and Optimus. All the bots
were feeling worse for wear after that
tumble.

As soon as Drift's treads touched solid
ice, Jetstorm leaped off his master and
started looked for his fellow Mini-Con,
Slipstream.

"Brother!" Jetstorm yelled. "Where are
you, brother?"

Windblade rushed to shush the
distraught Mini-Con. "Shhhh! We'll find
your brother, little guy, but we can't risk
triggering another avalanche. We need to

check our volume for the rest of the climb. That means you, too, Slick."

Sideswipe turned away, hiding his guilty expression.

Jetstorm pulled out his nunchucks and hacked at the snow and ice, digging wildly to try and find his brother. The other bots joined in, searching the surrounding area. Minutes passed without any sign of Slipstream.

"Don't worry, Jetstorm," Sideswipe said, moving snow away in huge handfuls. "You guys are tough little bots. A little tumble like that couldn't hurt Slipstream." But Jetstorm ignored Sideswipe's attempts at reassurance.

After a few more minutes of digging, Drift, mentor to both Mini-Cons,

sheathed his sword and whispered

something to Jetstorm.

The other bots

watched as Jetstorm's

expression turned

from panic to

disappointment and

finally to something like

resignation.

"I have spoken to my student," Drift

said to the group. "He understands that

our mission takes priority. I have

personally trained Slipstream and trust in

his ability to survive until we make our

way back down the mountain."

Optimus moved to protest. "We don't

leave bots behind, Drift. I'm field

commander, and I say we don't move

forward until everybot moves forward."

Before Drift could argue, Jetstorm stepped up. "Master Drift is right, sir. My brother would not want to jeopardise the mission. With all respect, I ask that we hurry to our goal and then return to find Slipstream."

Optimus didn't like what he was hearing, but looking up at the climb still to come — including the ground they had lost during their fall — he knew they had to push forwards. He latched on to the nearest handhold and led what was left of his team back up the mountain.

Meanwhile, a few hundred feet away on another side of the summit, Slipstream poked his head out of the snow and peered around. During the avalanche, a falling chunk of stone had sent him spinning away from the other bots. He had used his staff to slow his descent, preventing him from dropping into a crevasse or careening down the entire mountain.

"Jetstorm?" Slipstream asked tentatively. "Master Drift? Sideswipe?" The Mini-Con turned around and around, spotting no one. "... Anybot?"

For a nanocycle, Slipstream felt panic setting in. Then he remembered Master Drift's teachings. Slipstream folded himself into a meditative pose. He shut out the rushing wind and focused his thoughts on his situation.

*Either you've been separated from
your brother, your master and the other
bots or they've been trapped and you're
on your own to complete the mission,* he
thought. *If you have been separated, the
bots will know to carry on with the
mission. You can meet them at the top of
the mountain. And if they have been
trapped or captured, it is your duty to
defeat Abominus alone!*

Before he could
press on with his
mission,
Slipstream heard
a voice
somewhere
behind him. The
other bots!

Slipstream rushed toward the direction of the voice, down a slope from where he just landed.

"I told you, if we go off-trail, I'm not legally responsible for what happens to you!" a human voice said. Slipstream swallowed his disappointment and ducked behind a snowbank. With his winter camouflage, he easily blended into the scenery.

"And I told you, if I don't get some decent footage, the show is getting cancelled. Who knows if the studio will even bother paying the rest of your fee!"

From his hiding spot, Slipstream saw that there were three humans: a large man with a big moustache leading the way; a man with an artificial tan in the

middle; and an older fellow lugging a
camera bringing up the rear. All three
had heavy packs strapped to their backs
and looked various kinds of miserable.

"If you're going to threaten my
paycheque, I'll leave you right here now,"

the man with the moustache said. At this, the older cameraman looked worried.

"Uh, boss," he whispered to the man in the middle. "Maybe we should listen to Brigadier Wilson and just stick to the path. My camera has a real nice zoom; we can still get your footage."

The man in the middle looked ready to explode.

"Fine! We'll just rename the show *The Final Days of Loren Fortean with me, your soon-to-be-unemployed host, Loren Fortean!*"

Slipstream's suspicions were correct – it was the humans Rusty had told them about!

"Fine!" the man they called Brigadier Wilson whisper-shouted. "You want to go off-trail so badly, I'll take you – under two conditions. One: no more yelling. We're getting into avalanche territory, and I'm not going to dig you out if you bring half the mountain down on us."

"Fine," Fortean responded. He looked huffy, like a child who wasn't getting his way.

"And two: if we get footage of your mythical yeti, or anything else unusual, you pay me double."

"Double!" Fortean shouted at the top of his voice. Wilson shot him a dangerous look. "Double?" Fortean asked again, remembering to whisper.

"Double. Or I turn around now." Brigadier Wilson crossed his arms, refusing to budge.

"Fine, double – if we get footage that will help me save my show."

The two humans shook hands over their new terms and resumed their hike. Slipstream dug into the snow out of their sight. They might be on the hunt for strange creatures, but Slipstream was determined not to be their new movie star!

CHAPTER EIGHT

"DO WE HAVE TO DRIVE ALL THE way back through the woods?" Strongarm whined. Rusty Clay sat in the passenger seat of her police cruiser as they drove along at a mere five miles per hour. "I just want to relax."

"Yeah, me too!" Grimlock complained from his position hidden in the trailer behind them.

"You're not even walking, Grim," Strongarm replied. "I'm the one pulling a trailer with a new stasis pod and a whining Dinobot."

"Gosh, you Autobots sure can complain," Rusty said.

"They remind me of when you were a

toddler who didn't get his nap time – talk about fussy!" Denny Clay said from the passenger window of Bumblebee's vehicle. "I guess the only thing worse than a lazy Autobot is a lazy Autobot being forced to rev up and roll out."

After Fixit gave Rusty and Denny a crash course in Brakepad's energy-sapping powers, Rusty devised a plan to take down the Decepticon and free his friends from their lazy mood. Now if only he could get the bots to speed up!

"Can't you guys go a little faster?" Rusty pleaded. Strongarm responded by slowing down even further. "At the rate we're going, Brakepad will make it back to Cybertron before we catch up to him," Rusty sighed.

Strongarm revved her motor and pulled ahead. "Fine, I'll go faster, even though you're making me carry everything in the trailer. Who knew being an Autobot would be so exhausting ...?"

After a laborious trek full of complaining, Rusty and the others arrived at the crashed stasis pod that had once held Brakepad. Rusty leaped out of Strongarm's passenger seat with his backpack on. "OK, Dad, I'm going to look around—"

"No way, kiddo," Denny interrupted. He stepped out of Bumblebee with a bag of his own. "Slow or not, Decepticons are too dangerous. Help Strongarm unload the stasis pod while Bumblebee and I take a look around."

"What about me?" Grimlock asked.

"You just keep relaxing, Grim," Rusty replied. The Dinobot looked pleased with this response, while Bee and Strongarm changed back into their robot forms.

Denny asked Bumblebee to hoist him up on to his shoulder so the pair could look around more easily. The Autobot and his human companion walked a slow circle around the malfunctioning prison pod before Denny spotted their target.

"Bee, look up there!" Denny pointed to a tall chunk of wreckage sticking out of the ground. Brakepad was high overhead, clinging on to the wreckage with his massive claws. As he hung high up in the air he was slowly chewing a piece of metal debris.

"So what do you want me to do about it?" Bumblebee responded. "I'm here, and he's way up there."

"That Decepticon has energy-sapping powers," Denny explained, trying to figure out a way to persuade the laziness-afflicted Bumblebee into action. "If we don't take him down, he might take all your energy. That doesn't sound very relaxing, does it?"

Bumblebee grumbled in agreement.

"Rusty, how's that stasis pod looking?" Denny shouted to his son.

Rusty was sitting on Strongarm's shoulder, directing her as she pulled the pod off the trailer inch by inch. "Almost there! Hurry it up, Strongarm. You heard my dad, if we don't capture this bot, he might make you do work like this all the time."

"No way, I need my rest cycle!" the cadet responded. Once the pod was fully off the trailer, Strongarm shuffled her treads to join Bumblebee near Brakepad's hanging spot.

"Hey, you!" Rusty yelled up at the lounging bot. "We're taking you down!"

Brakepad stirred slightly in his perch. He turned his head around to stare at the squeaky human who was interrupting his rest. "Whoa, no need to shout. You're ruining my zen."

"Quick, Autobots, attack!" Denny commanded from his place on Bumblebee's shoulder. The bots were slow to respond. They half-heartedly raised their arms to swing at Brakepad, but the Decepticon had more than enough time to pull himself out of harm's way.

"Bummer, bro-bots, I thought you were cool," the Decepticon said. Brakepad's eyes started to flash. But before he could affect Bumblebee and Strongarm again, Rusty and Denny burst into action.

"Now!" Rusty shouted. He yanked an oversized pair of novelty sunglasses out of his bag and placed them snugly over Strongarm's optics. The lenses were sloppily painted, but they were black enough to block out Brakepad's energy-sapping vision. Denny did the same to Bumblebee.

The Autobots staggered back. "What gives?" Bumblebee asked.

"Don't take them off!" Rusty replied. "They're … relaxation glasses! They're protecting you from Brakepad's powers, so he can't take your energy!"

"Not cool, little dude," the Decepticon responded. "How am I supposed to chill them out now?"

"Grim, kick that stasis pod over here!" Rusty yelled. The Dinobot stirred slightly and then returned to relaxing. "If you don't, Strongarm said she won't pull your trailer. You'll have to walk all the way back to the scrapyard," Rusty added.

At the threat of too much labour, Grimlock stood up and gave the pod one massive kick. It slid through the grass and came to a stop in front of Brakepad's perch.

Denny tapped the blinkered Bumblebee on his arm to show him where to turn. "One last effort, Bumblebee! Just knock this guy loose and you can power down

until pigbots fly!" Rusty directed
Strongarm towards the same goal.
Gathering what little effort they had in
them, Bumblebee and Strongarm
pounded Brakepad's
perching spot and
shook the
Decepticon
loose. He
landed with
a *THUNK!*
in the new
stasis
pod below.
"Got him!" Rusty
shouted. He leaped off Strongarm's
shoulder and landed on the button that
closed and locked the stasis pod.

Brakepad was captured!

Denny climbed down Bumblebee's arm and high-fived Rusty. "Fantastic plan, son! Although I'm sad to see these vintage novelty glasses get ruined ..."

"Thanks, Dad," Rusty replied. "Now we just have to motivate these bots to drag the pod back to the scrapyard!"

CHAPTER NINE

THOUSANDS OF MILES AWAY AND thousands of feet up in the air, Slipstream made his way ahead of Loren Fortean's crew, rushing from hiding place to hiding place. Without knowing it, the humans had been walking straight up a booby-trapped path!

The diminutive Mini-Con had been darting ahead of them, defeating hidden dangers left and right to make sure the humans had an uneventful climb. Luckily for Slipstream, the sounds of his staff smashing turrets and slicing trip wires were covered by the raging winds.

"Start filming any dense flurries of snow," Loren Fortean commanded.

"We can run it later and say we saw a
shape disappear into it, drum up some
mystery." Fortean swallowed hard and
whispered to himself, "At this rate, the
bigger mystery will be where I can find
my next paycheque."

He and his crew were a mere hundred
feet from Slipstream, but the visibility
was so low that they couldn't tell! This
suited Slipstream just fine; there was less
of a risk of him being discovered.

Before long, Slipstream reached a
forking path. To the left, he spotted the
now-familiar signs of buried traps. To the
right, the snow looked clear. Quickly,
before the humans could catch up, he
used his staff to smash the rocks on the
left, collapsing the path so the humans

couldn't follow him. With a quick leap over the rubble, Slipstream found himself one step closer to finding Abominus, without the burden of babysitting the humans!

On the other side of the summit, Optimus and the Autobots neared the conclusion of their trek. They'd defeated countless traps and had been making good time to compensate for their fall earlier, but losing Slipstream had put them all in a dark mood. Not even Sideswipe could muster a joke.

As Everest's highest peak came into view, Optimus's treads clinked against something hidden under the snow.

"Hold up, team," the Autobot leader commanded. "I think I found something." Optimus bent down and brushed away the snow to reveal a door embedded in the rock!

"This must be an entrance to Abominus's lair," Windblade said, examining the door. "Drift, Slick, our blades can probably get it open." The three bots drove their swords into the heavy metal and pulled. With a serious effort, the door popped off its hinges, revealing a naturally occurring tunnel into the mountain. "That was probably the easy part. Expect Abominus to have plenty of other surprises waiting for us inside."

One by one, the bots filed inside.

Jetstorm brought up the rear, casting one final glance around for any sign of Slipstream. The bots' optics took a moment to adjust to the lack of light. The tunnel curved and led down a dark passageway.

"Is it strange that I'm nervous because we haven't run into any traps yet?" Sideswipe whispered.

"That's a smart instinct, Slick," Windblade responded. "Abominus isn't one to go light on the weaponry. There should be a lot more resistance down here."

As if on cue, Windblade's treads
landed on a pressure-sensitive tile. Panels
on the walls around them shifted,
revealing sharp spikes.

"Run!" Windblade shouted. The spikes
began shooting out of the wall in
unpredictable patterns, ricocheting
around the tunnel. Windblade, Drift,
Jetstorm and Sideswipe had no problem
dodging the projectiles thanks to their
acrobatic skills. Optimus, on the other
hand, was too slow and bulky to evade
them all.

Windblade rushed to the Autobot
leader's side as the spike barrage finally
subsided. "Optimus, are you injured?"
Windblade asked, even though she
already knew that Optimus wouldn't

admit to an injury, especially if it might jeopardise the mission at hand.

"The spikes flew right past me," Optimus said, but he winced as he stood up. "If that's the best Abominus can throw at us, he's going to be saying goodbye to his mountain sooner than he expected."

"Good thing that's not all I've got, eh?" a voice roared through speakers embedded in the rock. Suddenly, the floor below the bots retracted, sending them plummeting down another tunnel!

The bots landed with a *CLUNK!* Sideswipe was the first to stand up and take in his surroundings. The fall had dropped the bots in the middle of Abominus's lair – right into a cage!

Before Sideswipe could leap up, the roof of the cage slid into place.

"Trying to muscle in on my territory, are you?" Abominus said, stepping into view. The long-limbed Decepticon was shockingly white against the grey rock walls. A snowy environment was the perfect place for him to hide.

"Can't be having that, oh no! A bot's home is his castle, and I aim to defend mine."

"You're a wanted fugitive, Abominus!" Windblade shouted at their captor. "I'm going to put you back in stasis."

Abominus whistled in response. "Oh, ho, ho, tough-bot behind bars, eh?"

Windblade reached for her weapon, but before it left its holster, Abominus stepped towards a nearby console. "Oh no, can't have that!" With one press of a button, the cruel Decepticon sent thousands of volts rushing through the cage.

The Autobots grimaced and contorted in discomfort. "Not this again!" Sideswipe said. "I've got enough charge today to last – oof! – a millennium."

"Plenty more where that came from!" Abominus threatened. "But if you bots behave yourselves, I'll let you have front-row seats to my grand finale."

Optimus threw himself against the massive bars of the cage. "What are you talking about, Decepticon?"

"The little lifeforms of this planet insist on climbing up my mountain and building

their homes at the base of it," Abominus explained. "I've been placing explosives in key places all over the peaks. Once I've finished building the rest of these Energon bombs, I'm going to trigger them all at once and set off the avalanche to end all avalanches. *Boom!* No more intruders!"

m>
119
m>

CHAPTER TEN

"THIS IS BAD, TEAM," OPTIMUS SAID to his fellow bots.

"Yeah, no kidding, big guy," Sideswipe replied. "Abominus is probably going to strap us to those bombs when he blows up half the mountain!" Windblade and Optimus glared at the younger bot. "Plus, you know, all the humans who'd be caught in the avalanche ..."

"Any luck working on the bars, Drift?" Windblade asked. After revealing his sinister plan, Abominus had left to place more explosives around the summit, trusting his reinforced cage to keep the Autobots contained.

"Unfortunately, no," Drift replied.

"Every time my blade touches the cage, it – ahh! – electrifies." The samurai Autobot recoiled from the shock and placed his weapon back in its scabbard.

"And it's too risky to shoot my blaster in here," Optimus added. "The electrified forcefield could send the blast ricocheting back at us."

"I'm running out of ideas," Windblade said. "Abominus is dangerous. If he thinks blowing up half the mountain will help keep him isolated from outsiders, he'll do it. He wants to be left alone with only his weapons for company."

Sideswipe pointed at one of the video

screens nearby. "Looks like Abominus might have another unexpected guest to deal with, then." Through the grainy video, the bots could just make out Slipstream wandering through the tunnel!

A few nanocycles later, Slipstream tumbled down the same hole in the floor that had deposited the bots in their cage. With the roof now in place, the Mini-Con bounced off the top of the cage with only a momentary shock. He landed nearby, free from Abominus's trap.

"Brother!" Jetstorm and Slipstream shouted simultaneously. Slipstream noticed his master, too, and regained his composure. "Master Drift," he added with a bow. Drift nodded his head slightly in return.

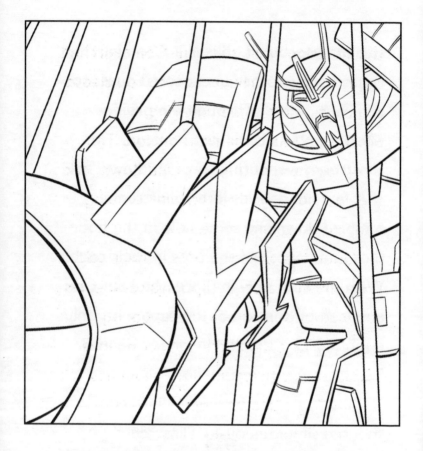

"I am glad you are safe," Drift said.

"Yeah, now get us out of here!"
Sideswipe added.

Optimus got Slipstream up to speed on

the situation while the Mini-Con searched
the consoles nearby for a way to release
the cage. After some tinkering,
Slipstream found the right button. The
electrical hum of the bars died down, and
the roof receded into the wall. One by
one, the Autobots climbed out.

"Good job, Slipstream," Optimus said.
Freed from the cage, Optimus took in his
surroundings. Half-assembled booby
traps lay all around the bots in various
states of construction. "OK, team, it's
time to lay our own trap ..."

Some time later, Abominus returned to
his lair. He glanced at the bots in their
cage and was satisfied to see them

locked away as he had left them. The orangutan-like Decepticon shook great mountains of snow off his back and sat in front of his wall of monitors.

"Soon enough I'll have the whole mountain to myself! No law-bots to bother me!" Abominus mumbled to himself. "The ultimate fortress! Eh, wait, what's this?" One of the Decepticon's camera feeds showed Slipstream entering the tunnel again!

"There's another one of your brain-rusted Autobots in my lair!" Abominus shouted. "Sit tight while I go and deal with your friend." Abominus swung himself up into the tunnel using his massive arms. He didn't notice that the Autobots' cage was no longer pulsing with electricity …

The moment Abominus left, Slipstream darted out from under a pile of half-built turrets. "The looped video worked – he thinks I'm still in the tunnel!" he declared. Slipstream retracted the roof of the cage. The bots quickly climbed out and dashed to the nearby consoles, just as they'd planned.

As Windblade hacked into the explosives' controls and disabled the Energon bombs placed around the mountain, the other bots watched Abominus barrelling through the tunnels. While he was gone, they'd had time to reprogram his many booby traps to target only one bot: Abominus himself!

Through the video feed, the Autobots

cound see Abominus being blasted by his
own turrets, swarmed by his own
nanodrones and tripped up by his own
hidden wires. If the video feeds had sound,
they'd probably be hearing a lot of rude

Cybertronian words, too!

"Man, after the climb we had getting here, watching this Decepticon fall for his own traps makes me feel like a million credits!" Sideswipe exclaimed.

"I deserve a million credits for this speedy hacking job," Windblade piped up. "There, all the Energon bombs have been disabled."

"Good job, Windblade," Optimus said. "Now it's time for the most satisfying trap of all." The Autobot leader pressed a big red button on the command console. Within nanocycles, the bots heard a fast-approaching scream and a *THUD!* as Abominus landed in the cage. The roof slid shut, and the bars jumped to life with electricity, trapping the Decepticon.

"Don't worry, Abominus," Windblade said, taunting the bot through the bars. "You're going to an isolated stronghold where no one will ever disturb you – a stasis pod!"

While the other bots worked on getting Abominus into a more permanent cage, Sideswipe glanced at the monitors. To his surprise, Loren Fortean and his crew had found their way to the mouth of the tunnel!

"Hey guys, looks like we have a few more visitors," Sideswipe said. "Rusty's TV guy made it up here! But don't worry, I've got a plan ..."

Back at the scrapyard, Rusty settled down in front of his television. It had taken a while to get Bumblebee, Strongarm and Grimlock back home with the captured Brakepad in tow, but by the time they arrived, the Decepticon's laziness effect had largely worn off.

Grimlock plopped down next to Rusty in front of the TV. "I feel so recharged!" the Dinobot exclaimed. "Maybe we can let that Decepticon out every once in a while for a spa day or something."

"I don't think so, bro-bot,'" Bumblebee said, joining his

team-mates. "I can't believe we were so lazy. Strongarm is out doing extra training just to make up for it. At least the Decepticon is safely in stasis now. He can 'chill' until we find a way to return him and the other escaped prisoners to Cybertron."

Rusty tried to quieten his Autobot pals. "That's great, you guys, but it's been an exhausting day, and I just want to watch *Beyond the—*"

"Great newt ... noon ... news!" Fixit proclaimed, hurrying to join the bots and Rusty. "I just heard from Optimus and the others. They have successfully captured Abominus and are making their way down the mountain."

"What about Loren Fortean and his

crew?" Rusty asked.

"Looks like you're about to find out," Fixit replied, pointing to the screen.

"That's right, faithful audience," the figure on the screen said. "My name is Loren Fortean, and I'm live-streaming from my climb down Mount Everest. Just moments ago, we brought you the very first verified audio recording of a real, live yeti! Play it back for everyone just tuning in, Ernie."

Rusty leaned forward, eyes glued to the screen and ears alert.

"WOOOOOOO, LEAVE THIS PLACE!" the recorded voice boomed.

"Wait a minute, I recognise that voice," Rusty said. "That's Sideswipe!"

"LEAVE MY MOUNTAIN AND NEVER

RETURNNNNN!" the voice went on.
"HI, RUSTYYYYYYY!"

Rusty gave a huge smile. The screen
cut back to Loren Fortean.

"That's right, dear viewers. I, Loren
Fortean, am the first person to capture

the mysterious sounds of the yeti on tape.
I'm not sure who this 'Rusty' is, but you
can bet I'll be investigating it – because my
show has been renewed for three more
seasons!"

Rusty turned to the others and grinned.
Now that was what he called a happy
ending!

··· MISSION COMPLETE ···

THE AUTOBOTS RETURN IN THEIR NEXT THRILLING ADVENTURE, DINOBOT DISASTER

READ ON FOR A SNEAK PEEK!

CHAPTER ONE

GRIMLOCK BASHED THE ENEMY BOT. *SMASH!* It flew away and bounced off the wall of the control room, landing in a crumpled heap. A second bot charged at him. He waited for the right moment then flipped his huge tail around in a great arc, slapping the enemy away. It sailed into a bank of computers, landing with a flash of sparks and a crackle of energy.

But there were more enemy bots all around. Small and grey with vicious weapons clustered all over them, they raced towards Grimlock from every direction. The Dinobot stood tall and roared, ready for the battle. Suddenly one of the bots made a piercing, high-pitched wailing sound. Grimlock blinked at it in surprise as it started talking to him ...

"... Autobots! Action Stations! Alan ... Albert ... ALERT!"

Grimlock woke up on top of a huge pile of old, dented cars, trying to work out what was happening. Gradually he realised it wasn't an enemy bot talking to him! It was Fixit. He'd been dreaming about smashing bots and now he was awake. He sat up and peered over the side of the pile.

Woken by Fixit's cries, the other Autobots sprang into action as well. First came Bumblebee, the leader, a yellow sports car, flashing across the scrapyard, heading for the command centre. Strongarm, in the form of a police car, roared out of her bay. Next, racing from his garage, came the sleek red racing car that was the vehicle form of Sideswipe.

**READ
DINOBOT DISASTER
TO FIND OUT WHAT
HAPPENS NEXT!**

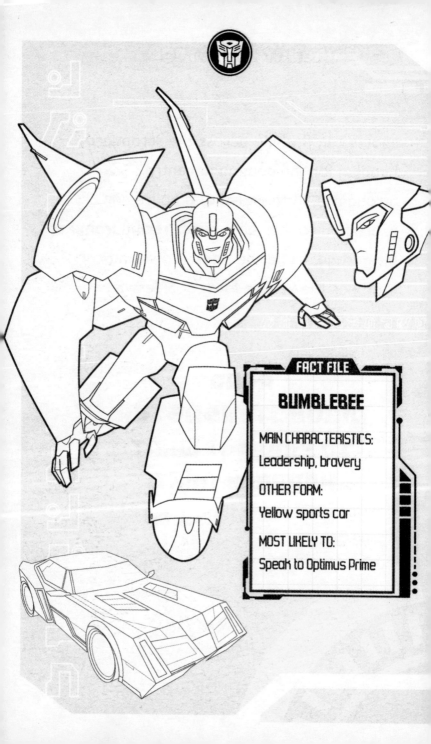

FACT FILE

BUMBLEBEE

MAIN CHARACTERISTICS:
Leadership, bravery

OTHER FORM:
Yellow sports car

MOST LIKELY TO:
Speak to Optimus Prime

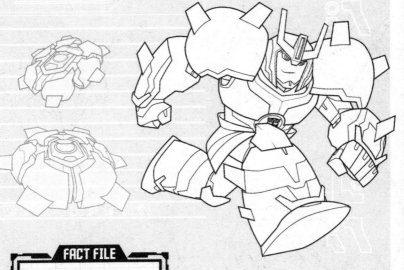

FACT FILE

MINI-CONS

NAMES:
SLIPSTREAM, JETSTORM

MAIN CHARACTERISTICS:
Loyalty, speed

MOST LIKELY TO:
Listen to Drift

FACT FILE

GRIMLOCK

MAIN CHARACTERISTICS:
Strong and misunderstood
former Deceptican

OTHER FORM:
Dinobot

MOST LIKELY TO:
Run away from cats

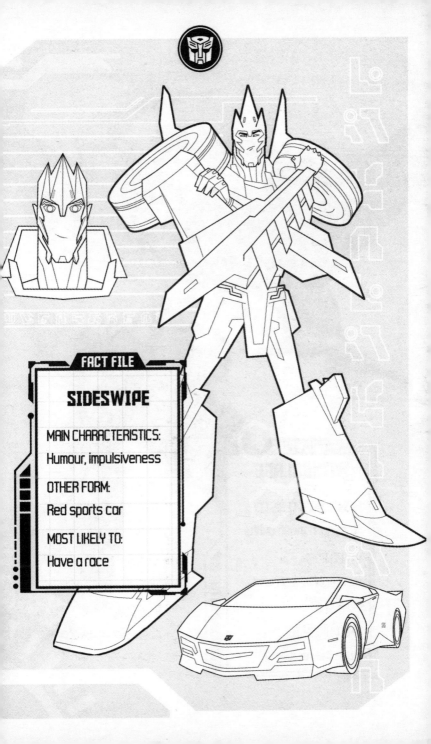

FACT FILE

SIDESWIPE

MAIN CHARACTERISTICS:
Humour, impulsiveness

OTHER FORM:
Red sports car

MOST LIKELY TO:
Have a race

FACT FILE

WINDBLADE

MAIN CHARACTERISTICS:
Trusting, honest, dutiful

OTHER FORM:
A vertical takeoff and
landing jet

MOST LIKELY TO:
Fly to the rescue